18

Mirror-Belle

and the Flying Horse

**Books by Julia Donaldson
illustrated by Lydia Monks**

The Princess Mirror-Belle series
Princess Mirror-Belle
Princess Mirror-Belle and the Magic Shoes
Princess Mirror-Belle and the Flying Horse
Christmas with Princess Mirror-Belle

Picture books
Princess Mirror-Belle and the Dragon Pox
The Princess and the Wizard
The Rhyming Rabbit
Sharing a Shell
The Singing Mermaid
Sugarlump and the Unicorn
What the Ladybird Heard
What the Ladybird Heard Next
What the Ladybird Heard on Holiday

Plays
The What the Ladybird Heard Play
The What the Ladybird Heard Next Play

★ JULIA DONALDSON ★

TWO
BOOKS
IN ONE

Princess
Mirror-Belle
★ and the Flying Horse

Illustrated by

★ LYDIA MONKS ★

MACMILLAN CHILDREN'S BOOKS

These stories previously published 2006 in *Princess Mirror-Belle and the Flying Horse* and in 2015 in two separate volumes as *Princess Mirror-Belle and the Flying Horse* and *Princess Mirror-Belle and the Sea Monster's Cave* by Macmillan Children's Books

This edition published 2017 by Macmillan Children's Books
an imprint of Pan Macmillan
20 New Wharf Road, London N1 9RR
Associated companies throughout the world
www.panmacmillan.com

ISBN 978-1-5098-3890-5

Text copyright © Julia Donaldson 2006
Illustrations copyright © Lydia Monks 2006, 2015

The right of Julia Donaldson and Lydia Monks to be identified as the author and illustrator of this work has been asserted by them in accordance with the Copyright, Designs and Patents Act 1988.

Princess Mirror-Belle

and the Flying Horse

For Alyssa

Contents

The Flying Horse 5

The Magic Ball 51

The Flying Horse

"There!" said the nurse with the blue belt, looking proudly at the hard white plaster on Ellen's right arm. "All ready for your friends to write their names on it."

Ellen had fallen off her bike and broken her arm, and Mum had taken her to hospital. The arm wasn't hurting nearly as much as it had at first, and Ellen liked the idea of her friends writing their names on the plaster.

"Can I go back to school tomorrow?" she asked eagerly.

"No," said the nurse. "The doctor wants you to stay in hospital tonight, just so we can keep an eye on you. It's because you had concussion."

"What's that?"

"It's when you bang your head and forget things."

It was true that Ellen's head had hit the pavement when she fell off her bike, and for a minute or so she hadn't been able to remember where she was or what had happened.

"I'm always telling her to wear her cycle helmet," said Mum to the nurse.

Ellen looked at the floor and felt guilty. "Sorry," she muttered. "But I feel fine now."

"All the same, we need to keep you in to be on the safe side." The nurse turned to Mum and added, "I expect you'll be able to take her home tomorrow, after the doctor's done his ward round."

A porter appeared with a wheelchair. "Sit in this, old lady," he said to Ellen, and, "You'll have to walk, young lady," to Mum.

It seemed strange to Ellen that she should need a wheelchair when it was her arm and not her leg that she had broken,

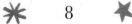

8

but she was too shy to say so. The porter wheeled her in and out of a lift and then along a corridor into a room with six beds in it.

"This is Jupiter Ward," he said. "You'll get five-star treatment in here." He parked the wheelchair at the reception desk.

A nurse with a red belt welcomed Ellen and Mum. "I'm Sister Jo," she told them. She showed Ellen her bed, which had a curtain you could draw all round it. Then she fitted a plastic bracelet on to Ellen's left wrist. It had her name on it.

"You'll need to put these on too." Sister Jo was holding out some hospital pyjamas.

"But how will I get the top on over the plaster?" Ellen asked.

"Don't worry – we think of everything,"

 9

said Sister Jo. When Mum helped Ellen put the pyjamas on they found that the right sleeve had been cut off and the armhole widened so that the plaster could fit through it.

"I'd better go back home now," said Mum.

Ellen felt a bit scared. "I don't want you to go," she said.

"You'll be fine. It's only for one night. And I'm sure you'll make friends with the other children."

But looking around Jupiter Ward, Ellen could see only one other child, a boy who was asleep. Three of the beds were empty and the other one had its curtains drawn around it.

"Hardly anyone seems to be breaking any bones these days," said Sister Jo. "If it wasn't for you, Ellen, I might lose my job!"

Ellen smiled, and found she felt less scared. She hugged Mum goodbye with her left arm and made her promise to bring in a bunch of grapes and a library book the next day.

"Now, down to business," said Sister Jo when Mum had gone. "You need to choose what you want to eat tomorrow. Are you left-handed by any chance?"

"No," said Ellen, puzzled. "Do you do different meals for left-handed people then?"

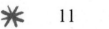

Sister Jo laughed. "No – but it might be a bit difficult for you to fill this in." She showed Ellen a card with some writing on it. "It's got the different food choices for breakfast and lunch," she said.

Ellen chose cornflakes and orange juice for breakfast, and chicken pie and fruit salad for lunch. Sister Jo ticked the boxes for her.

"I'm going off duty now," she said. "I'll be back tomorrow lunchtime, but you might be gone by then."

Ellen was sorry to see Sister Jo go. Another nurse took her temperature, and then a different one brought her some cocoa and yet another one took her to the bathroom. It was bewildering having so many different people to look after her and Ellen suddenly felt tired. One of the nurses tucked her up in her new bed.

"Just ring this bell if you want anything in the night," she said.

Ellen was woken by a light tap on her shoulder. At first she thought it was Mum, but then she opened her eyes, saw the nurse and remembered where she was. Although she hadn't felt ill enough to ring the bell, it hadn't been a good night. Because of the plaster she couldn't sleep on her right side like she usually did, and it was hard to find a comfortable position. Then she had been woken up very early to have her temperature taken, after which she had fallen into a much deeper sleep.

"We couldn't wake you up when the breakfast trolley came round," the nurse said now. "But don't worry – we've saved yours for you. You should have time to eat it before Doctor Birch comes."

"Have I got time to go to the bathroom too?" asked Ellen.

"Yes. Do you want someone to come and help you?"

"No, thanks." But once Ellen was in the bathroom she found it was quite awkward washing and cleaning her teeth with only her left hand.

"I'll have to learn to write left-handed too," she said aloud.

"That's a good idea," came a voice from the bathroom mirror. "Who knows? That way you might start doing the letters the right way round at last."

Ellen knew that voice very well. It belonged to Princess Mirror-Belle.

Princess Mirror-Belle looked just like Ellen's reflection, but whereas most

 15

reflections stay in the mirror, Mirror-Belle had a habit of coming out of it. Although she looked like Ellen, she was not at all like her in character. Ellen was quite shy, but Mirror-Belle was extremely

boastful and was full of stories about the palace and the fairy-tale land she said she came from.

Mirror-Belle was dressed in hospital pyjamas just like Ellen, but her plaster was on her left arm.

"Well, don't just stand there staring," she said. "I'll need a bit of help getting out of here." She stuck her right arm out of the mirror and added, "Don't pull too hard. I don't want to break this one as well."

Although Ellen wasn't really sure that she wanted Mirror-Belle in hospital with her, it seemed too late to change things, so she grasped her hand and helped her to wriggle out on to the washbasin and down to the floor. "Did you fall off

 17

your bike too?" she asked.

"Certainly not," replied Mirror-Belle. "Would you expect a princess to ride around on anything as common as a bicycle? No . . ." She hesitated for a second and then went on, "I fell off my flying horse."

"You never told me you had a flying horse."

"Well, I'm sorry, Ellen, but I can't tell you all the things I have. It would take too long and it would just make you jealous."

"Were you wearing a riding hat?" asked Ellen. But Mirror-Belle wasn't listening. She had opened the bathroom door and was sauntering into Jupiter Ward.

Ellen was about to follow her, but then decided to hang back. Somehow

she couldn't face trying to explain to the nurses about Mirror-Belle.

She peeped out of the bathroom door and saw her mirror friend climbing into her own bed and ringing the bell above it.

One of the nurses came scurrying to her bedside.

"What is this food supposed to be?" Mirror-Belle asked, pointing to the

breakfast tray on the table beside her bed.

"It's what you ordered. Cornflakes and orange juice."

"Cornflakes? What are they? Take them away and bring me a lightly boiled peacock's egg."

The nurse tittered. She seemed to think this was a joke.

"Don't laugh when I'm giving you your orders," said Mirror-Belle. "It's very rude. You can take the orange juice away too. I'd rather have a glass of fresh morning dew with ice and lemon."

"You're not getting anything else," said the nurse. "Anway, the breakfast trolley's gone now."

"Then call it back again this second."

The nurse picked up the untouched breakfast tray and scurried off with it, nearly bumping into a man in a white coat with a stethoscope round his neck. Ellen guessed that he must be Dr Birch.

"I think she's taken a turn for the worse," murmured the nurse with the tray.

The doctor went over to the bed and drew the curtains round it. Ellen, still peeping out of the bathroom, couldn't see him any longer, but she heard his voice.

"It's Ellen, isn't it?" the doctor was saying.

"No, it's Princess Mirror-Belle. I hope you're properly trained to look after royalty. That stethoscope looks very ordinary. The palace doctor has one made of silver and snakeskin."

Dr Birch chuckled. "My little niece likes playing princesses too," he said. "Very well, Your Royal Highness. Now, I want you to tell me everything you can remember about your accident. I see from your notes that you fell off your bike."

"Then your notes are wrong," said Mirror-Belle. "I fell off my flying horse. I'm a very good rider, actually, so I can't quite think how it happened. I suspect that my wicked fairy godmother was up to her tricks again – loosening the saddle or something."

"So you have no memory of any bike ride? Maybe that's because you banged your head on the pavement."

"I did no such thing!" said Mirror-Belle indignantly. "There aren't any pavements where I live. I landed . . . um . . . in a stork's nest on the palace roof. Luckily there weren't any stork's eggs in it at the time, otherwise—"

"Just a minute!" interrupted the doctor. His voice sounded quite different suddenly – urgent and excited. "It says

here that you broke your right arm."

"I do wish you'd stop reading those stupid notes and listen to me instead," complained Mirror-Belle.

"It's not just the notes. The X-ray shows it quite clearly too. The right arm was broken, but they've plastered the left one!"

"It sounds as if you should sack the plasterer as well as the note-taker."

"How does your right arm feel? Does it still hurt?"

"Now you mention it, it is a little sore. I think that must be from where the storks pecked it. They didn't realize who I was, you see. They probably thought I was a cuckoo who was about to lay its egg in their nest."

Doctor Birch obviously wasn't interested in storks or cuckoos, because Ellen saw him emerge from behind the curtains, almost run to the reception desk and pick up the telephone. His back was turned and Ellen could only catch a few words, such as "mistake", "urgent" and "emergency". She guessed that he was speaking to someone in the plaster room.

This had gone too far, Ellen decided. She really ought to explain everything to

the doctor and nurses. She was just braving herself to stride out from the bathroom when she saw someone familiar come into Jupiter Ward. It was the same porter who had wheeled her there yesterday, and he was pushing an empty wheelchair.

"You again, old lady?" she heard him say to Mirror-Belle.

Ellen didn't think Mirror-Belle would like being called "old lady" and expected her to tell the nice porter off, but instead Mirror-Belle answered, "Ah – at least someone recognizes that I'm not just an ordinary little girl. And I'm delighted to see that you've brought this splendid throne for me. Even the palace thrones don't have wheels!"

"Nothing but the best for you, old lady,"

26

said the porter, and he wheeled her out of Jupiter Ward.

Oh dear! Ellen had to stop this. If Mirror-Belle's left arm really was broken, it wouldn't do for the plaster to be taken off.

Maybe the easiest person to explain things to would be the nice porter. Ellen stepped out of the bathroom and glanced around the ward. The doctor was talking to the nurse at the reception desk. They were gazing deeply into each other's eyes and didn't notice Ellen as she slipped out of the ward. She was just in time to see the porter pushing Mirror-Belle into a lift.

"Stop!" she cried, but the doors had already slid closed.

There was another lift and Ellen pressed the button to call it. It took a long time to come, but at least it was empty when it arrived, so no one could give her funny looks or ask what she was doing on her own.

If the plaster room was where her own arm had been plastered, Ellen was pretty sure it was on the ground floor, so she pressed the G button. But when the lift stopped and she got out, there was no sign of Mirror-Belle or the porter. Ellen found herself in a long corridor with lots of doors leading off it. She looked at the notices on some of the doors but they weren't much help because she couldn't understand what the words meant: one said "Endocrinology", another said "Haematology" and a third "Toxicology". Ellen was just wondering whether one of these "ology" words was a special medical way of writing "plaster room" when the Haematology door swung open and a nurse with a purple belt came out.

"Can I help you?" she asked Ellen. She looked and sounded quite kind.

"I'm looking for the plaster room," said Ellen.

"Isn't anyone with you? Where have you come from?"

Ellen hesitated, wondering what to tell the nurse. She decided on the truth, even though she doubted if she would be believed.

"I've come from Jupiter Ward," she said, "but they don't know I'm here. You see, they thought my friend Princess Mirror-Belle was me. The thing is, Mirror-Belle broke her left arm but—"

"Just a minute," Purple Belt interrupted her. "Perhaps I'd better phone Jupiter Ward and see what's going on." She took Ellen to an office with a phone in it.

"I think I've got a patient of yours

 30

here." Purple Belt took Ellen's left hand and read the identity bracelet round her wrist. "She's called Ellen Page, and she says she's supposed to be in the plaster room . . . That's all right then; I just wanted to check, because she  seems a bit confused . . . talking about princesses and things like that . . . oh, I see – concussion; yes, that would fit . . . No, it's OK, I can take her there myself."

Purple Belt put down the phone and smiled brightly at Ellen. "They offered to send another porter, but it's only just round the corner," she said. She took Ellen to a door with a couple of chairs outside it.

Ellen knew she was in the right place

because she could hear a familiar voice from inside the room: "My horse's name is Little Lord Lightning. Unfortunately he's been suffering from wing-ache recently. I really ought to take him to the palace vet."

Purple Belt smiled at Ellen and rolled her eyes. "You might have a bit of a wait. It sounds as if there's quite a difficult patient in there."

Ellen decided against saying, "It's Princess Mirror-Belle." Purple Belt would just think she was still confused. Instead she answered, "I don't mind waiting."

"Goodbye then," said Purple Belt. "You won't wander off, will you?"

"No," promised Ellen, sitting down on one of the chairs. She watched Purple Belt disappear down the corridor. Now that she had tracked Mirror-Belle down she found she was dreading the idea of barging into the plaster room and explaining everything to the nurse in there.

"That's funny," came a voice from the room, interrupting Mirror-Belle's account of her flying horse. "I can't read the name on your bracelet. The letters look kind of back to front. I'd better go and get my reading glasses – they're in my coat pocket." A nurse came out of the room. It wasn't the same one who had put Ellen's arm in plaster, though she had a blue belt like hers.

The nurse hurried down the corridor and Ellen, relieved at this chance to talk to Mirror-Belle on her own, slipped into the room.

Mirror-Belle was standing by the window, holding a large pair of scissors in her right hand. "Oh, hello, Ellen," she said. "Do you think these scissors are really suitable for cutting a royal plaster? They look rather poor quality to me. I thought I might try them out on a few things myself before the servant returns." She aimed the scissors at the curtains.

"Stop!" cried Ellen. She grabbed the scissors from Mirror-Belle. "The nurse will be back in a second and you've got to go!" she told her.

"Don't you start ordering me around, Ellen," Mirror-Belle reproached her. "You're getting to be as bad as your servants. I'll come and go as I please."

"But surely you don't want to stay and have your plaster cut off? If you've broken your arm, you need it."

"Good point," said Mirror-Belle. "Now you're talking sense. Perhaps I should go back and see how Little Lord Lightning

 35

is getting on. Besides, no one here seems to have any respect for royalty – except for the throne-pusher, that is. He was extremely polite. I might see if I can find a job for him in the palace."

"Mirror-Belle, just go – please!" Ellen begged.

"All in good time," replied Mirror-Belle. She picked up a pen from the table.

"What are you doing now?" Ellen felt rattled. Everything would be so much easier if Mirror-Belle had gone by the time Blue Belt came back.

In reply, Mirror-Belle held the pen out to her. "As a special honour, I'm going to allow you to be the first person to sign my plaster," she said.

There was obviously no wriggling out of this, so Ellen took the pen and wrote her name as well as she could with her left hand.

"Really, Ellen, this is even worse than your normal writing. As well as being backwards, the letters are awfully wobbly."

"They're not backwards – and they only look wobbly because I'm writing left-handed."

"I'll show you how it should be done," said Mirror-Belle, taking the pen from

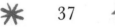

Ellen. She wrote her own name on Ellen's plaster. It looked like this:

Mirror_Belle

"Talk about backwards and wobbly," Ellen couldn't help muttering, even though there wasn't time for an argument. She glanced round the room, hoping to see a mirror, but there was none.

Just then they heard footsteps in the corridor. Blue Belt was coming back!

"Farewell!" cried Mirror-Belle, and she darted out of the door. Ellen peered out and saw her go through a door on the other side of the corridor. It had another of the long "ology" words written on it. "Ophthalmology," this one said.

"Now, now," said Blue Belt, coming into

the plaster room. "You were supposed to stay sitting down. It's funny," she added, "I thought for a moment that I saw you going into the eye department, but it must have been someone else."

She put on her reading glasses and looked at Ellen's identity bracelet.

"That's good – I can read it fine now," she said. "Ellen Page." She checked the name against Ellen's notes, and then frowned. "There's no problem with the name, but I can't understand what the doctor's written. It says, 'Remove plaster from left arm and plaster right arm,' but your right arm is plastered. I suppose he must mean, 'Remove plaster from right arm and plaster left arm'."

"No, no!" exclaimed Ellen in alarm. "It's the right one that's broken. The left one works fine." She waved it about to prove her point.

Blue Belt checked the notes and the X-ray.

"Well, it's all very strange," she said. "I do wonder if that Doctor Birch's mind is always on his work."

She phoned for a porter to take Ellen back to Jupiter Ward and then frowned again. "It's funny," she said, "but I could have sworn the plaster was on your left arm too! Before I fetched my glasses, that is. I really ought to pop into the eye department and get my sight checked."

At that moment there was a babble of voices in the corridor and someone knocked on the door. Blue Belt opened it, and Ellen heard three voices speaking at once. As far as she could make out, a woman was asking, "Is she in here?" and a boy was saying, "I keep telling you what

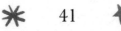 41

happened," and a man was saying, "Be quiet, Toby."

"I'm sorry – who are you looking for?" asked Blue Belt.

"I don't even know her name, but I thought she might have been one of your patients," came the woman's voice. "I was just checking little Toby's eyesight – you know, that test where they have to read the letters in the mirror – and this girl with her arm in plaster came charging in. She was talking a lot of nonsense, something about all the letters being back to front. She refused to leave when I asked her to, so I went to get the doctor to help me, but when we got back she'd just disappeared."

"Yes – into the mirror!" came the boy's voice.

"Don't be silly, Toby. You know that's impossible," said the man.

"But I saw her!"

"Yes, but don't forget you need new glasses."

"Well, I'm sorry," said Blue Belt, "but whoever she is, she's not in here."

Ellen had found a blanket and covered herself with it, terrified that the people outside would come in, see her and accuse her of Mirror-Belle's bad behaviour. But they seemed happy to accept what Blue Belt said, and she heard the woman saying,

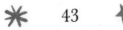

"Maybe she belongs on Jupiter Ward. I'll try phoning them."

Blue Belt shook her head when they had gone. "Everybody seems to be going mad today," she said. "Except you, Charlie," she added to the nice porter who had just come into the room.

"Hello, old lady – has that naughty nurse been drawing pictures on your plaster?" he said to Ellen. Ellen smiled faintly and sat down in the wheelchair.

"You've gone all quiet," he told her as he pushed her into the lift. "Aren't you going to tell me any more stories about your flying horse?" Ellen just shook her head and closed her eyes. She suddenly felt very tired.

Back in Jupiter Ward, two friendly

people were there to greet her – Sister Jo and Mum. Mum was looking quite worried. "I hear you've been a bit delirious," she said.

"No, I'm fine," said Ellen.

"If you ask me," said Sister Jo in a low voice, "it's that Doctor Birch who's been a bit delirious. Fancy not knowing his right from his left! I think he must be in love. I'm going to ask Doctor Hamza to see you as soon as you've had your lunch. You must be starving – I gather you didn't fancy your breakfast."

"That's not like you, Ellen," said Mum.

Ellen, who didn't feel like explaining, gobbled up her chicken pie and fruit salad. She was halfway through the bunch of grapes that Mum had brought in when Dr Hamza appeared at her bedside. He asked her about her fall and got her to count backwards from a hundred to fifty.

"She seems very fine and dandy to me," he told Mum. "You can take her home."

Mum had brought in some new clothes, including a blouse with a cut-off sleeve like the hospital pyjama top. She helped Ellen into them.

"Do you want to pop into the bathroom before you go?" asked Sister Jo. "Then you can see in the mirror how smart you look."

"No!" said Ellen. "I mean, no, thank you. Can I go back to school now and show everyone the plaster?"

"That can wait till tomorrow," said Mum. "I think you should take things easy this afternoon. You can finish the grapes and read the new library book I've got out for you."

"What's it called?" asked Ellen.

"*The Flying Horse*," said Mum, and couldn't understand why Ellen laughed all the way down in the lift.

The Magic Ball

"Don't get too many yellow cards, Ellen!" said Dad.

Ellen's big brother Luke chortled at this, but Ellen just smiled thinly. "I might not even play football," she said. "There are lots of other sports you can choose."

The leisure centre was having an open day. Dad and Luke were going to play a game of squash, and Ellen was doing something called "Four for Free", which

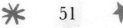

meant you could try out four sports without paying anything.

"We'll be on squash court three," said Dad. "Just in case you need me to sort out any refs for you!" he added.

Luke chuckled again. "I think I'd better do that, Dad. You won't be in a fit state after I've beaten you!" Then the two of them strode off, swinging their rackets jauntily.

Ellen decided to try out the Eight and Over gym first. It didn't have any weight-lifting machines like the big gym, but it did have a trampoline and some running and cycling machines.

She showed her Four for Free card

to the muscular young attendant in the gym. He ticked one of the boxes on it and handed it back to her.

The gym was very busy but Ellen found a free running machine. She'd never been on one before so the attendant had to show her how to use it.

It felt strange at first to run on the spot. Ellen was just getting the hang of it when she heard a voice saying, "You're going the wrong way!"

Ellen had been concentrating so hard on her feet and the

little screen showing her speed that she had hardly taken in the row of mirrors facing the running machines. Startled by the voice, she stopped running.

Her reflection stopped just as suddenly – except, of course, that it wasn't really her reflection; it was Princess Mirror-Belle.

"Mirror-Belle! What are you doing here?" asked Ellen.

Princess Mirror-Belle jumped off her machine and jogged out of the mirror and into the gym. "Chasing the magic ball," she said. "Have you seen it?"

Ellen looked round. She couldn't see a ball, and she was relieved that no one else in the gym seemed to have noticed Mirror-Belle; they were all too busy bouncing and running or cycling.

"What magic ball?" she asked.

"The one my wicked fairy godmother threw," said Mirror-Belle. "She's been up to her tricks again. She's turned everyone in the palace to stone."

"Except for you," remarked Ellen.

"Yes, well, she was going to do it to me too, but luckily I knew the special magic words to stop her."

"What were they?"

Mirror-Belle looked rather annoyed, and said, "Don't hold me up – I told you, I have to find the magic ball."

"You still haven't explained about that," said Ellen.

"Haven't I? Well, the wicked fairy threw it and said that the stone spell would

only be broken if I could bring it back to her. You should have heard her cackle!"

"Why was she cackling?"

"Because everyone knows that it's almost impossible to keep up with her magic ball. I've  been chasing it for days – through forests and up and down mountains – but it's always just ahead of me. And now I seem to have lost sight of it altogether."

Mirror-Belle glanced round the gym and then her eyes lit up. "Aha!" she said,

and she marched up to the muscular attendant.

"You can't fool me," she told him, and she jumped up and tapped his arm.

"Stop mucking about," he said.

"That's no way to talk to a princess," said Mirror-Belle. "And, in any case, you're the one who's mucking about. Roll up your sleeve immediately!"

"Stop it, Mirror-Belle," said Ellen. "You'll get us chucked out."

"But it's perfectly clear he's hiding the magic ball up his sleeve," said Mirror-Belle.

"Don't be silly – that's not a ball, it's just

58

his arm muscles," said Ellen, laughing.

The attendant looked quite amused and actually did roll up his right sleeve. He was probably glad to have a chance to display his bulging biceps.

Mirror-Belle looked unimpressed and demanded to see the other arm. But by now the attendant had had enough. Perhaps he thought they were trying to make fun of him.

"Why don't you two buzz off and try out something else," he said. Then a suspicious look crossed his face. "Have I ticked both your cards?" he asked.

Ellen showed him hers, and Mirror-Belle also took a card from the pocket of her tracksuit trousers. The attendant stared at it. "That's funny," he said. "The

writing's all wrong on this one."

Ellen glanced at Mirror-Belle's card. She was not surprised to see that it was in mirror-writing. Instead of saying FOUR FOR FREE it said:

ꟻOUꓤ ꟻOꓤ ꟻꓤEE

"It's perfectly correct," said Mirror-Belle. "You probably just left school too young, before you'd fully mastered the art of reading." She shook her head and turned to Ellen. "All muscles and no brain," she murmured. Ellen couldn't help giggling.

The attendant was really cross now. "Get out!" he said.

Ellen tugged at Mirror-Belle's arm. "Why don't we have a go at five-a-side football?" she said.

"Football, did you say? That sounds promising!"

To Ellen's relief, Mirror-Belle seemed to forget about the muscular attendant's left arm and she followed Ellen out of the gym and down the stairs.

In the five-a-side hall a woman in a pink tracksuit looked pleased to see them.

"Good – we needed an extra two to get started," she said. "I hope you don't mind being on different teams." After hurriedly checking their cards, she gave Ellen a blue armband and Mirror-Belle a red one and told them where to stand. Then she put a football down in the middle of the pitch.

Mirror-Belle looked disappointed. "That's not the magic ball," she said. "It's too big, and it's the wrong colour. I'll

61

have to search elsewhere."

"Oh, do stay," said Ellen. "Otherwise your team will be one short."

Mirror-Belle shrugged her shoulders. Pink Tracksuit blew a whistle, and everyone started running around, kicking the ball and trying to score goals.

One of the other children on the red team passed the ball to Mirror-Belle and she picked it up. "Thank you," she said, "but it's no use to me. Here, Ellen, catch!" And ignoring Pink Tracksuit, who was blowing her whistle, she threw the ball to Ellen.

The others on the red team started shouting at Mirror-Belle.

"Stupid!"

"You're not allowed to use your hands."

"She's on the other side anyway."

Mirror-Belle looked shocked. She went up to Pink Tracksuit. "Excuse me – you seem to be in charge. What is the punishment for being rude to royalty? In my father's kingdom these people would have to weed the palace gardens for a year."

Pink Tracksuit ignored this. "Free kick for the blues," she announced and, "Get back in your place," she told Mirror-Belle.

"Just who do you think you are?" Mirror-Belle asked her.

"I'm the coach," said Pink Tracksuit.

Mirror-Belle started to laugh. "In that case, where are your six white horses? Where are your wheels and your velvet cushions? Where are the driver and the footmen?"

Pink Tracksuit looked as if she might send Mirror-Belle off, and Ellen tried to come to the rescue. "I'm sorry," she said. "I don't think she's ever played football before." She managed to coax Mirror-Belle back on to the pitch. "You have to kick the

ball, and only to people in your team – or into the goal," she told her. "That's the net thing," she added, pointing, as Mirror-Belle was looking blank.

Pink Tracksuit blew the whistle and the game started up again. The blue team scored a goal, and then another one. Then the reds got the ball. One of them passed it to Mirror-Belle.

"No – not to her," moaned another red player, but it was too late. Mirror-Belle had given the ball a huge kick. It landed in the red team's goal.

"Yes!" shouted some of the blues,

jumping up and down, but the reds were furious.

"You idiot!"

"That was an own goal!"

"Get her off!"

Once again Mirror-Belle strode up to Pink Tracksuit. "I'm simply not putting up with this petty jealousy," she complained.

"We're not jealous!" said one of the reds.

"Yes, you are. I've just done what those two other people did – kicked the ball into the net – but, if I may say so, with far greater skill and style than they did. I can't help it if the rest of you can't match up to me."

"But it was the wrong goal! You should have kicked it into the blue goal!"

"Really," said Mirror-Belle, "I can't be bothered with all these silly details. You'll just have to play four-a-side. Come on, Ellen, let's go."

Ellen thought this was a good idea, and so did everyone else.

"Well, that was a waste of time," said Mirror-Belle as they left the football hall. "Now maybe I'll never find the magic ball, and my parents and all the servants will remain statues for ever. I suppose in that case I'd have to come and live with you, Ellen."

Ellen wasn't too sure

about this plan. A little of Mirror-Belle went a long way. Luckily she was saved from replying because Mirror-Belle stopped suddenly outside a door and said, "Just a minute, do I hear bouncing? What's in there?"

"It's the indoor tennis courts." Tennis was one of the sports you could choose as part of Four for Free, although after the football experience Ellen wasn't keen for Mirror-Belle to join in.

But she had no choice. Mirror-Belle had already opened the door, and a jolly-looking woman in white shorts and a T-shirt was greeting them.

"Hi there, four-for-frees! Jolly good – now we can play doubles; what fun!" She gave them both tennis rackets and

introduced them to two other girls called Jade and Ailsa. Then she asked Ellen, "Do you two want to play together or opposite each other?"

"Together," said Ellen hastily, remembering the disastrous football game.

A lot of yellow tennis balls were lying on the ground and Mirror-Belle was inspecting them. "These are the right colour, but they're too furry, and they're not trying to escape," she said.

The jolly woman laughed heartily. "Now, how about a little knockabout before you start a proper game?" she suggested. "You serve first, Mirror-Belle."

"Naturally," said Mirror-Belle. She picked up a ball and hit it to Ellen.

Jade and Ailsa giggled, and the jolly woman said, "Whoopsadaisy!"

"You're not supposed to pass it to me," said Ellen.

"Why ever not? You're on my team, aren't you?"

"Yes."

"Well, in that other stupid game you said I was to pass the ball to people on the same team. Which is it to be? Do make up your mind – I haven't got all day."

"Well, you see . . ." Ellen was about to explain the difference between football and tennis when Mirror-Belle's face lit up. "Oh, I understand!" she said, and picked up the ball. This time it hit

the net. "Goal!" she cried.

Jade and Ailsa giggled some more, but the jolly woman said, "Don't laugh at her. She's doing her best." Then she turned to Mirror-Belle. "Try hitting it a little higher and you'll get it over all right."

"But surely it wouldn't be a goal if it went over the net?" said Mirror-Belle.

"You don't score goals in tennis," Ellen told her. "You have to keep hitting the ball over the net till the other side can't manage to hit it back."

"Well really, this is too tiresome for words. Things are so much simpler back home. When I play with my own golden ball I just throw it and catch it – there's none of this nonsense about teams and goals and nets and red and blue.

Occasionally, of course, the ball falls into a pond, but then it usually gets rescued by a frog and I turn him into a prince by kissing him."

The jolly woman laughed again, more uncertainly this time. "I tell you what," she said. "I think you two would enjoy putting. That's quite a straightforward game."

"That's a good idea," said Ellen, but only as a way of getting out of the embarrassing tennis game. She didn't really want to try another sport with Mirror-Belle, and once they were outside in the corridor she said, "Maybe the magic ball has bounced back

to your land, Mirror-Belle. Don't you think you ought to go back and look for it there?"

"No, I'm sure it's here somewhere." They had reached the reception area and Mirror-Belle looked around. "What about this butting game? Is there a ball in that?"

"It's putting, not butting," said Ellen, alarmed by the thought of Mirror-Belle trying to head-butt a golf  ball. "Yes, there is a ball, but . . ."

A receptionist overheard them. "Do you want the putting green? Go out through the main door and turn left," she said, and the next second Mirror-Belle was

 73

prancing eagerly outside. Ellen followed her doubtfully.

The attendant on the putting green gave them each a club and a ball. Ellen was relieved to find that they could play by themselves, without having to join another group of children.

Mirror-Belle looked disappointed with her ball. "There's nothing magic about this," she said, but she was intrigued by the metal flags sticking out of the ground, each one with a number on it.

"How curious," she said. "At home we fly the flag of the kingdom high above the palace. It has a lion and a unicorn on it – except that by now I suppose the wicked fairy must have taken it down and replaced it with her own horrible flag."

"What's that got on it?" asked Ellen.

"Er . . . a spider and a centipede," replied Mirror-Belle. "Still, even that's a bit better than these silly flags in the ground."

"But these ones are different. They're just for the game – to show you where the holes are," Ellen tried to explain.

Instead of listening to her, Mirror-Belle was swinging her golf club about experimentally, as if it was a tennis racket.

"No, not like that. You have to put the ball on the ground, then hit it."

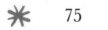

75

"Get a move on, can't you," came a voice from behind them, and Ellen saw that three boys were queuing up to have a game.

Feeling flustered, she said to Mirror-Belle, "Why don't I go first, so I can show you? I'm not very good, mind."

She stood with her feet apart, swung her club back and gave the ball a smart tap. To her surprise it ended up really near the hole. With a bit of luck she should get it in with the next shot. Ellen felt quite pleased with herself and hoped that the impatient boys were impressed.

But what was Mirror-Belle up to? Instead of placing her own ball on the ground she was running after Ellen's one. And now she was whacking it back in Ellen's direction –

except that it went sailing past her and hit one of the impatient boys.

"What do you think you're doing?" he yelled, clutching his knee.

"Returning the ball, of course," said Mirror-Belle. "And it was a pretty good shot, if you ask me. Ellen here didn't

manage to get it back – that's one point to me."

"No, it's not!" Ellen found herself shouting at Mirror-Belle. "I wish you'd listen to me. This isn't tennis, it's putting. It's like golf – you have to get the ball down the hole."

"Well, really!" Mirror-Belle sounded loud and indignant too. "I must say, I thought better of you, Ellen. You keep making me play these stupid games when you know I should be looking for the magic ball, and then you change all the rules to suit yourself."

"No, I don't. And I don't want you to play with me anyway. It was your idea."

"I thought you were my friend," said Mirror-Belle. For the first time ever, Ellen thought she could see tears in her eyes. But she couldn't be sure because the next second Mirror-Belle had thrown down her club and was running away, back towards the main doors of the leisure centre.

"What a nutcase," said the boy with the hurt knee. One of the others seemed to feel sorry for Ellen. "You can play with us if you like," he offered.

"No, it's all right. I'd better make it up with her."

Ellen returned the clubs and balls to the

attendant and then followed in Mirror-Belle's footsteps.

"Have you seen my friend?" she asked the receptionist.

"Oh, I thought she was your twin. Yes, she was here a minute ago. She looked a bit upset. She went into the crèche."

Ellen's heart sank. The crèche was only supposed to be for toddlers and very young children; they could stay there and be looked after while their parents played sports or went to the gym. What on earth was Mirror-Belle up to in there?

She found out as soon as she opened the door and a lightweight blue ball hit her, followed by a red one.

Mirror-Belle was in the ball pool, hurling the balls out of it at a frantic speed. A few

excited toddlers were copying her and some others were running around outside the ball pool, picking up the balls and throwing them around. Everyone seemed to be having a good time except for the two women in charge of the crèche. One of them was telling Mirror-Belle off; the other one, seeing Ellen coming in, looked up from the nappy she was changing and said, "Is that girl in the ball

pool your twin? Can you tell her to stop throwing the balls around?"

"She's not, but I'll try," said Ellen and went up to the ball pool.

"Ah, Ellen, there you are at last!" Mirror-Belle greeted her in a friendly voice.

She seemed to have forgotten about their quarrel. "Do you know, that wicked fairy  is even more cunning than I thought. She's obviously sent the magic ball in here and she thinks I won't be able to find it among all the others. But I'm sure I'll recognize it. For a start, a lot of them are the wrong colour." She threw a green ball out. "And so far none of the yellow ones feel right. They don't bounce properly." She hurled a couple of yellow balls in different directions. One of them landed softly on the tummy of the baby whose nappy was being changed. He clutched it and burbled happily.

"I expect the magic ball has sunk to the bottom," went on Mirror-Belle. "I'll probably have to get rid of all the others before I find it."

"Mirror-Belle, you've got to stop that! You're not supposed to be in here anyway."

"Who said so? I don't notice any kings or queens around here and they are the only ones who can tell princesses what to do or where to go," said Mirror-Belle.

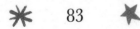

"But you're too old for the crèche," said Ellen.

"In any case, you have to be signed in by your mother or father," added one of the crèche-workers. She was wearing a badge with a smiley face and the name Tracy on it.

Mirror-Belle looked at her as if she was an idiot. "That's impossible," she said. "As I've already told you, both my parents have been turned to stone."

"Fwo! Fwo! Fwo!" shouted a toddler, eager for some more action. He clamped his arms round one of Mirror-Belle's legs. Obligingly, Mirror-Belle threw a few more balls out of the pool.

Tracy turned to Ellen, hoping to get more sense out of her. "Where are your

parents?" she asked.

"Well, my dad's on squash court three," Ellen admitted. "But he's not *her* father," she added hastily.

"Fwo! Fwo!" the toddler started to clamour again, but Mirror-Belle ignored him. "You never told me your father had a court like mine," she said to Ellen in surprise. "How many courtiers does he have waiting on him?"

"It's not that sort of court – not a royal one," said Ellen. "Dad's playing squash with Luke."

"Oh," said Mirror-Belle,

appearing to lose interest. She threw a few more balls around, but rather half-heartedly. Then, all of a sudden, she unclamped the demanding toddler from her leg and sprang out of the ball pool. "I think I've been on the wrong trail all the time," she announced. She ran to the door, flung it open and was gone.

Several little children tottered after her and started crying when Tracy closed the door. The demanding toddler grabbed Ellen's leg and started up his chant of, "Fwo! Fwo! Fwo!" He seemed to expect her to start where Mirror-Belle had left off.

"I'm sorry about all that," said Ellen to Tracy.

"Don't worry," said Tracy. "We can't choose our families."

Ellen decided it would be useless to explain again that Mirror-Belle wasn't related to her. Instead she helped Tracy pick up the scattered balls and throw them back into the ball pool. The toddlers didn't seem to enjoy this nearly as much as they had enjoyed Mirror-Belle throwing them all out, and the crying grew louder.

"Well, I'd better go," said Ellen when the last ball was back in the pool. She wondered where Mirror-Belle had got to but decided not to look for her this time. She would go and find Dad and

 87

Luke on their squash court.

She didn't need to. As soon as she opened the door she saw them outside in the corridor.

"So that's where you've been hiding," said Dad.

Luke was looking cross. "Give it back," he said.

"What are you talking about?" asked Ellen.

"The squash ball, of course. That yellow one was our best one. It was really bouncy."

"But I haven't got it."

"Then what have you done with it?"

"Nothing. I never had it."

"Yes, you did – you came rushing in and snatched it."

"It wasn't me. It must have been Mirror-Belle. She was looking for the magic ball, you see – the one her fairy godmother threw – and—"

"Oh shut up." Luke turned to Dad. "She's always telling whoppers."

But Dad was in a surprisingly good mood. "Ellen's got a vivid imagination, that's all," he said. "And it's not as if that yellow ball was ours anyway. We just found it on the court when we arrived."

Luke didn't want to give up so easily. "She's hidden it in the kids' gym somewhere," he said. "I'm sure I saw her go in there."

Ellen guessed that Mirror-Belle had run back to the gym with the squash ball – or was it really the magic ball? In either case, she had probably taken it back to her own land through one of the mirrors in the gym. But Ellen knew that to say so would be the wrong thing. It would only make Luke even crosser. So instead she asked, "Who won at squash?"

Luke scowled. That seemed to be the wrong thing too.

"I did," said Dad.

Princess Mirror-Belle
and the Sea Monster's Cave

For Gaby

Contents

The Sea Monster's Cave 97

The Unusual Pets Club 137

The Sea Monster's Cave

"For goodness sake," said Ellen impatiently to her big brother, who was pushing yet another coin into his favourite seaside slot machine. "I bet Granny and Grandpa wouldn't want you to waste all their money on that thing."

"I'm not wasting it. I'm going to end up with more than I started with." Luke's teeth were gritted and his eyes had a determined gleam. "Can't you see, that

whole pile of coins is about to tumble off the edge. Then I'll win them all! I'll probably win them next go." But he didn't; or the next go or the one after that.

They had been on holiday for a week, staying in a caravan park with their grandparents. Granny and Grandpa had gone out for a last row in their boat and had given Luke and Ellen ten pounds spending money each.

"I'm sick of hanging around waiting for you," Ellen complained. "At this rate I won't get to the shops at all. Don't forget, they're taking us out this afternoon, and tomorrow we're going home."

"Well, why don't I see you back here in an hour," suggested Luke, and Ellen agreed, even though she knew he had promised to look after her.

There were two gift shops by the beach. Ellen wandered round one of them and chose a packet of sparkly pens and a little notepad with a picture of a seal and "Best wishes from Whitesands" on the front. She

paid for them and put them in her backpack, along with her sun lotion.

She still had six pounds left so she went into the second shop, which sold all sorts of ornamental sea creatures – fish, lobsters and sea horses – as well as boxes covered in shiny shells. Most things were too expensive, but Ellen enjoyed looking round. Tucked away in a corner she found a beautiful

mirror decorated
round the outside
with a mermaid and
shells. It cost £9.99,
and Ellen began
to wish she hadn't
bought the things in
the first shop. She

was just wondering whether she could take
them back when a voice from the mermaid
mirror said, "So it *is* you! I nearly didn't
recognize you under all those freckles." It
was Princess Mirror-Belle.

"Mirror-Belle!" Ellen hadn't seen her
mirror friend all holidays and felt quite
pleased to see her now, even though she
knew there was bound to be trouble ahead.
"You've got lots of freckles too," she said.

"Don't be silly – they're not freckles, they're beauty spots," replied Princess Mirror-Belle, and she dived out of the mirror, landing on her hands with her legs in the air.

The shop assistant must have heard the thud. She left the customer she was serving and hurried over to them, looking cross.

"Please don't do hand-stands in here," she said to Mirror-Belle. "You might break something."

"It wasn't a handstand. It was a dive," said Mirror-Belle, on her feet by now. "With all these sea creatures around, I naturally assumed I would land in the sea. It's extremely confusing; I suggest you remove them and put some land animals on the shelves instead."

"Why don't you go and play on the beach?" said the shop assistant.

"I didn't hear you say, 'Your Royal Highness'," objected Mirror-Belle, "but it's quite a good idea, so I'll excuse you just this once. Come on, Ellen."

"Sorry," Ellen murmured to the assistant, and she followed Mirror-Belle out of the shop and on to the beach.

Three children were digging in the sand. Mirror-Belle went up to them.

"I doubt if you'll find any treasure here," she said. "The sea monster is much

103

more likely to have hidden it in a cave, and he's probably guarding it."

The children just stared at her.

"They're not digging for treasure – they're building a sandcastle," Ellen told Mirror-Belle.

"What a ridiculous idea! You can't build a castle out of sand. I should know, I live in one."

"I thought you lived in a palace," said Ellen.

"That's in the winter. In the summer we go to our castle by the sea. It's made of pure white marble with ivory towers." Mirror-Belle turned back to the children. "In any case, you shouldn't build it on the beach. Don't you realize it will collapse when the tide comes in?"

"We don't mind," said one of them. "We'll have gone home by then."

"What? You're building a castle and you're not even going to live in it?" Mirror-Belle shook her head pityingly. "There's no hope for them, Ellen. We'd

better move on," she said.

"Shall we look for shells?" suggested Ellen as they walked along between the sea and the row of beach umbrellas.

Instead of answering her, Mirror-Belle gazed at the sky and then marched up to the nearest umbrella. A man and a woman were dozing underneath it.

"Allow me," said Mirror-Belle, and she stepped over them and closed the umbrella.

"Hey, what are you doing?"

said the woman, sitting up.

"What does it look like?" answered Mirror-Belle. "There's not a trace of rain, so you really don't need an umbrella."

The man was on his feet by this time. "Buzz off," he said as he opened the umbrella up again.

"I'm a princess, not a bee," replied Mirror-Belle.

Ellen tugged at her arm and Mirror-Belle allowed herself to be pulled away, but not without saying in a loud voice, "I'm beginning to wonder if this is a special beach for idiots."

"They're not idiots," Ellen told her off when they were out of earshot. "They just don't want to get sunburned. That reminds me, I ought to put some lotion

on." She took the bottle out of her back-pack. "It's to protect me against the sun," she explained, and then realized that Mirror-Belle had an identical bag on her back. "Haven't you got some too?"

"Not exactly," said Mirror-Belle, opening her own bag. Ellen looked inside and saw some sparkly pens and a notepad just like the ones she had just bought. Mirror-Belle took out a bottle and unscrewed the cap. "This is to protect me against sea monsters," she said as she smeared some of it over her neck and arms.

Ellen laughed. "I don't

think you get sea monsters in Whitesands," she said.

"I wouldn't be so sure," replied Mirror-Belle darkly. She screwed up her eyes and looked out to sea. "I can't see any," she admitted, "though I can see some rather ugly mermaids on that rock. Their tails look all right, but why haven't they got long golden hair?"

Ellen looked too and laughed again. "Those aren't mermaids – they're seals," she said.

"Well, give me mermaids any day," replied Mirror-Belle. "The rocks near our castle are covered in them."

"Do you play with them?" asked Ellen, though she wasn't really sure if she believed in these mermaids.

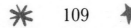

"Sometimes. It's not much fun though, because they spend so much time combing their hair." Mirror-Belle paused for a moment and then added, "One of them gave me a magic comb for my birthday."

"What was magic about it?" asked Ellen.

"It could change your hair into any style you wished for. The colour too. I once had purple ringlets down to my toes."

"Have you still got the comb?"

"Really, Ellen, I wish you wouldn't always ask so many questions. If you must know, it was stolen by a sea monster."

"Are sea monsters hairy then?"

"Of course. I thought even you would know that."

They reached the rocky end of the beach, where there were fewer people. They picked seaweed off the rocks and made necklaces with it and a crown for Mirror-Belle, who said, "It's a shame you can't have one too, Ellen, but the only way you could become a princess would be to marry a prince."

They wandered along the curved shore further than Ellen had ever been before. There were cliffs behind them now and

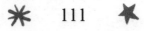

they had to clamber over boulders. They reached the tip of the bay and carried on into the next one.

"Look!" said Mirror-Belle, pointing to an opening at the foot of a cliff. "That's the entrance to a cave. I wonder if it belongs to the sea monster. Would you like some of my protective lotion, Ellen?"

"All right," said Ellen, just to keep Mirror-Belle happy. She was pretty sure that sea monsters didn't exist; at least, they might do in Mirror-Belle's world, but not here in Whitesands.

The cave, when they reached it, was disappointing. It was quite small and empty, except for a couple of cans and a lemonade bottle. "No sign of any sea monster," said Ellen.

"On the contrary." Mirror-Belle had picked up the empty lemonade bottle and was looking excited. "Didn't you know, they love lemonade? If they don't drink lots of it, they lose their slime."

"I thought you said they were hairy," Ellen objected, but Mirror-Belle didn't seem to have heard her. She was examining some writing on the wall of the cave. Ellen looked too and saw that a lot of people had carved their names into the rock. "Look at this!" said Mirror-Belle, pointing to some rather wiggly letters which said: "T. Box 1.8.01."

"What about it?" asked Ellen.

"Can't you see? It's a clue. The 'T' must stand for treasure."

"It probably stands for Tom or Tessa or

 113

something," said Ellen. "And Box is their surname."

"The poor creature has written it back to front," Mirror-Belle carried on, ignoring

Ellen, "but then sea monsters aren't very intelligent. Never mind – look at those numbers, Ellen: they're the important thing. They show us where the treasure box is buried."

"I think they're just the date," said Ellen. "'1.8.01' means the first of August, 2001. That's when this Box person carved their name."

"Nothing of the sort," scoffed Mirror-Belle. "It means that we have to take one step in one direction, eight steps in another direction and then dig one foot underground."

Ellen frowned doubtfully. This wasn't the first time Mirror-Belle had been so excited about treasure. Ellen remembered when she had claimed that her dog, Prince

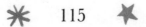

 Precious Paws, could sniff out gold and jewels, but he hadn't succeeded.

"Don't look so gloomy, Ellen," Mirror-Belle reproached her. "You should be even happier than I am! After all, I'm incredibly rich already, but think what a difference all this wealth will make to you."

This reminded Ellen of Luke and all the coins in the slot machine.

"Help!" she said. "I must go. Luke will be getting worried – and I expect Granny and Grandpa will be back by now. Are you coming?"

"Of course not. Can't you see, this is the perfect opportunity to dig up the treasure,

when the sea monster isn't guarding it."

"Do be careful, Mirror-Belle," said Ellen and then had to remind herself that sea monsters didn't really exist.

"Oh, I'll be fine. I've got my protective lotion, remember. But I'm surprised that you're leaving me to do all the digging by myself. Just think – there might even be a magic comb buried with all the gold and jewels. You'd like that, wouldn't you?"

But Ellen couldn't be persuaded. She hurried back over the rocks and along the beach. She found Luke pacing about outside the arcade of slot machines.

"Thank goodness you're back," he said. "They'd go mad if I'd lost you."

"Sorry," said Ellen. "I've been with Mirror-Belle."

"Oh, do shut up blaming everything on someone who doesn't even exist," Luke snapped at her. Ellen decided that now wasn't the best moment to ask him if he'd won any money, but from the expression on his face she doubted it.

That afternoon Granny and Grandpa took them out to a bird sanctuary, and they all had supper in a cafe on the way home.

"You're very quiet, Ellen, pet," said Granny.

"She's tired," said

Grandpa, but it wasn't that. Ellen couldn't help thinking about Mirror-Belle and hoping she was all right. Was she still in the cave or had she returned to her own world? Ellen half expected to find her waiting for them when they got back to the camper van, but she wasn't.

"Early to bed and early to rise," said Granny after the game of cards they always played in the evening. "We've got a long journey tomorrow."

But Ellen couldn't sleep. She lay awake in the camper van listening to her grandparents' gentle snores and worrying about Mirror-Belle. If only there was someone she could talk to! She wondered if Luke was still awake. He didn't sleep in the camper van but in a tent just outside.

 119

Ellen put her anorak on over her pyjamas and slipped on her shoes. Quietly she opened the door of the camper van and stepped outside. It was a clear night and the moon was nearly full.

"Luke!" she whispered. She unzipped his tent a few inches and whispered again. There was no reply. Ellen knew he would only be cross if she woke him. She really should go back to bed, but instead she found herself walking down to the little beach where

Granny and Grandpa moored their rowing boat.

She looked out to sea. She could see the cliffs at the end of the bay, but now the tide was high, covering the boulders where she and Mirror-Belle had clambered that morning.

The next bay, the one with the cave, must be cut off by the tide. If Mirror-Belle was still there, she would be trapped. Usually she escaped into her own world through a mirror, but there wasn't one in the cave.

A breeze blew in from the sea and Ellen shivered. She thought of Mirror-Belle with no anorak to keep her warm. She wouldn't have had anything to eat either. And if she really did believe in sea monsters, she

might be feeling scared as well as cold and hungry.

Then Ellen noticed something bobbing in the water. It was a plastic lemonade bottle. It looked as if there was something inside it: a scrap of paper.

Ellen rolled up her pyjama trousers, took a couple of steps into the cold water and reached out for the bottle. She unscrewed the top. Sure enough, there was a rolled-up piece of paper inside it. When Ellen unrolled it and saw the glittery backwards writing she knew at once who the message was from. This is what it said:

HELP! I AM TRAPPED IN THE SEA
MONSTER'S CAVE. I NEED A NICE PRINCE
TO RESCUE ME. THE REWARD WILL BE HALF
MY FATHER'S KINGDOM AND MY HAND IN
MARRIAGE (WHEN I AM OLD ENOUGH).

PRINCESS MIRROR-BELLE

XXX

Ellen was very good at reading backwards writing after all her adventures with Mirror-Belle, so she read it as:

HELP! I AM TRAPPED IN THE SEA
MONSTER'S CAVE. I NEED A NICE PRINCE
TO RESCUE ME. THE REWARD WILL BE HALF
MY FATHER'S KINGDOM AND MY HAND IN
MARRIAGE (WHEN I AM OLD ENOUGH).

PRINCESS MIRROR-BELLE
XXX

An hour later, Ellen and Luke were in their grandparents' boat. Luke was rowing. "This had better not be a trick," he said.

It had been easier than Ellen had imagined to wake her brother and talk him into this night-time rescue  operation. Luke had always liked adventures, and although he had never before believed in Mirror-Belle, the back-to-front note in the bottle had seemed to convince him.

"There's the cave!" Ellen pointed at the dark hole in the cliff face. She was relieved to see that there was a strip of sand in front of the cave; at least it wasn't flooded.

"Look!" She stood up and pointed again in great excitement.

"Sit down – you're rocking the boat," said Luke. He was rowing with his back to the cliffs and couldn't see what Ellen could see – a pale figure standing in the mouth of the cave.

"Mirror-Belle!" she called out.

A few minutes later Mirror-Belle was climbing into the boat.

"Hello, Ellen," she said, and then, "My prince! My hero!" she greeted Luke.

"He's not a prince. He's just my brother," said Ellen.

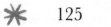 125

"Never mind. He will be a prince once he marries me, won't you, my brave rescuer?" She flung her arms round Luke, who wriggled awkwardly out of her grasp. One of her seaweed necklaces had come off and stuck to him and he threw it into the sea.

"Settle down, you girls," he said, and picked up the oars.

"It's a pity you didn't get the chance to slay the sea monster," said Mirror-Belle. "I can't think where he can have got to."

Ellen was surprised that Mirror-Belle was in such a perky mood after being trapped in the cave for so long. "Did you find any treasure?" she asked.

But Mirror-Belle only seemed to want to talk to Luke. "Which half of my father's kingdom would you like?" she asked him as the boat bobbed along. "One half is covered in mountains and the other half is full of deep lakes."

Luke didn't reply but Mirror-Belle was not put out. She picked up the lemonade bottle with the note in it from the floor of the boat. "My father might ask a few questions about you at first, but I'm sure

I can make him see reason if I show him this," she said.

Ellen was beginning to feel annoyed. "It was me who found that, you know, not Luke. I've been worrying and worrying about you."

But Mirror-Belle's mind was still full of the marriage arrangements. "I suppose we'll have to wait about ten years," she said to Luke. "You could be learning a few princely things in the meantime, like hunting dragons and cutting off trolls' heads. Would you rather do that here or would you like to come back with me and have some lessons in the palace?"

"I'm trying to concentrate on the rowing," said Luke. Ellen could tell from his voice that he felt embarrassed.

 128

"Luke doesn't want to get married," she told Mirror-Belle. "All he cares about is his band."

"That's not a problem," said Mirror-Belle. "He could be in a band of princes. They could be called the Dragon Slayers or the Royal Rescuers . . . or the Handsome Heroes." She turned back to Luke. "How would you like to play a golden guitar?"

"Am I just dreaming this?" Luke muttered.

They had reached the caravan park beach.

"I'll tie up the boat," said Luke as they clambered out. Mirror-Belle tried again to hug him, but he shrugged her off.

"Do you want to sleep in the camper van with me?" asked Ellen. "You'll have to be quiet, so as not to disturb Granny and Grandpa."

 But Mirror-Belle didn't like this idea. "I'll sleep under the stars," she said. "Then I can guard my hero's tent in case the sea monster comes to take revenge."

"You'd better have my anorak then," said Ellen.

Luke offered rather reluctantly to sleep outside himself and let Mirror-Belle have

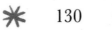

the tent but she refused. "You've been enough of a hero for one night," she told him. "It's my turn to be a heroine."

"Your tea's cold," said Granny to Ellen the next morning. "I've tried to wake you about five times."

Ellen sat up in bed and noticed that Granny was holding her anorak.

"I found this on the ground outside," she said.

"Was Mirror-Belle there?" asked Ellen. "She said she wanted to sleep under the stars."

Granny chuckled. "That's some dream you've been having."

Grandpa came in. "That's it – I've fixed the boat to the tow bar," he said. "I was

131

hoping that brother of yours would help me, but he's dead to the world."

"Shall we leave him behind, Ellen? What do you think?" joked Granny. But Ellen was thinking more about Mirror-Belle than about Luke. As soon as she was dressed she went outside to look for her. Luke was just staggering, bleary-eyed, out of his tent.

"Mirror-Belle seems to have gone," said Ellen.

Luke looked blank for a second and then scratched his head. "That's funny – I had a dream about Mirror-Belle," he said. "Something about a message in a bottle and rescuing her in a boat."

"It wasn't a dream. It was real!" Ellen protested. "I can show you the bottle and the message!" But then she remembered that Mirror-Belle had them. By now she must have taken them back through some mirror or other into her own world.

Grandpa appeared at the doorway of the camper van. "Good afternoon," he said to Luke, though it was only half past nine. "You'd better start taking that tent down. Everything else is packed up."

He gave the windows of the camper van a loving wipe and then made a tut-tutting noise.

"What's the matter?" asked Luke.

 133

"Someone's been fiddling about with the wing mirror. It's all bent back."

Grandpa straightened it out and then said, "That's funny."

"What is?" Ellen asked.

"There's seaweed all over it," said Grandpa. "I wonder how that got there?"

Ellen smiled to herself, but she said, "I can't think."

The Unusual Pets Club

"Do you want to come back to my house for tea?" Ellen asked her best friend, Katy. They were in the school playground.

"I can't. I'm going to the Unusual Pets Club."

"What's that?"

"I don't really know much about it. It's the first meeting tonight, at Crystal's house. Hasn't she asked you too?"

"No." Ellen felt cross. Crystal was a

bossy girl in their class who was always starting up clubs and societies and then meanly not letting everyone join.

"You have to have an unusual pet to join it," said Katy. "Maybe you could bring Splodge along. Shall I ask Crystal?"

Ellen didn't know what to say. She wanted to pretend that she didn't care about the stupid old club, but in fact it sounded quite fun.

Just then, Crystal came up to them.

"Hi, Katy," she said. "Do you know how to get to my house?"

"I think so," said Katy. "Can Ellen come too?"

Crystal looked doubtful. "Well, I don't know. I didn't think you had an unusual pet, Ellen."

 139

"She's got Splodge," said Katy. "He's a really nice dog. He's brilliant at chasing sticks and bringing them back, isn't he, Ellen?"

"But all dogs can do that," objected Crystal. "There's nothing unusual about it."

"What sort of unusual things do you mean?" asked Ellen. As far as she knew, Crystal's hamster, Silver, was perfectly normal.

But Crystal obviously didn't think so. "Well, like Silver, for instance," she said. "You know hamsters have two pouches in  their cheeks and they stuff food in them? Well, Silver only ever uses his right pouch, never the left one – it's amazing!"

"And Twiglet can do this sort of dance," said Katy. Twiglet was her stick insect, and it was true that sometimes he moved from side to side in quite a rhythmic way, whereas most stick insects stayed still all the time.

"I tell you what, Ellen," said Crystal graciously. "See if you can teach Splodge a trick or something after school, and then you can bring him along at six o'clock. But it will be a sort of trial. If he's not unusual enough then he can't come to any of the other meetings."

When Ellen got home she found her old hula hoop and took Splodge out into the garden. She held the hoop out in front of him and said, "Jump!"

But Splodge didn't understand; he just

sat looking up at her eagerly as if he expected her to throw the hoop for him. Ellen had to give up on that trick.

She didn't succeed any better when she tried to teach Splodge to stand up and beg, or to thump his tail three times when she asked how old he was. The only thing he would do was shake hands, but Ellen didn't think Crystal would call that unusual enough.

A spider scuttled over Ellen's shoe and suddenly she had an idea. Her brother Luke had a pet tarantula called Evilton. A tarantula would surely count as an unusual pet.

She ran into the house with Splodge at her heels. Luke was sprawled on the sofa watching the music channel on television.

"Can I borrow Evilton?" asked Ellen breathlessly.

"Be quiet – this is Fire Engine's new release." Luke turned the volume up and sang along with the band:

"So you think you can ride the storm, babe,
And there's nothing you can't do
But I can see a big wave coming
And it's gonna crash over you."

Ellen fidgeted impatiently till at last the song came to an end. Then she asked him again.

"Please, Luke. Just for this evening. I want to take him to the Unusual Pets Club."

"No," said Luke. "I'm not having Evilton join some silly girly club."

"It's not just for girls. Martin Booth is bringing his slow-worm. Oh, go on, Luke!"

"No," said Luke. "Evilton might catch cold. Anyway, I need him to help me with my homework!" He laughed as if this was hilarious, and when Ellen tried to argue he turned the volume up even louder. Fire Engine was singing another song.

Suddenly Ellen realized that she had missed most of her favourite programme,

Holiday Swap. She picked up the remote control, but Luke snatched it back.

"You're so mean," said Ellen. "This stuff is on twenty-four hours a day, and *Holiday Swap* only lasts half an hour."

"I got here first," said Luke, and he made her wait while the band was interviewed before he handed over the control. "OK – it's all yours," he said at last, and went out of the room, leaving the door open.

Ellen switched channels. *Holiday Swap* had just finished.

"I hate you," she shouted after Luke. She turned the television off angrily. Splodge laid his chin on her lap and she stroked his head. "You're the only nice one," she told him.

"What about me?" came a ghostly

whisper. The voice sounded slightly familiar, and for a moment Ellen wondered if it was Mirror-Belle. But there was no mirror in the room, and anyway the voice was too soft to be Mirror-Belle's.

Splodge had heard the mysterious whisper too, and he didn't like it. He whined and hid behind the sofa, leaving Ellen to stare at the television, which is where the voice seemed to have come from. And yet she had definitely turned

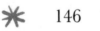

it off – the screen was dull and blank. Actually, that wasn't quite true: Ellen could just see herself in it, but it wasn't what she would call a proper reflection; it was faint and grey and transparent.

"Happy Throughsday," whispered the faint grey transparent person, and stepped out of the television.

"Mirror-Belle – it *is* you! But you look all funny – like a ghost! I can see right through you."

"Well, what do you expect on Throughsday?" said Princess Mirror-Belle.

✳ 147 ✭

Her voice was a little louder now, more of an eerie chant than a whisper.

"You sound funny too. And what do you mean – Throughsday? It's Thursday today."

"It may be Thursday here, but back home it's Throughsday," said Mirror-Belle. "Everyone can walk through things on Throughsday. Like this." And she walked through the sofa. Splodge growled.

"That's amazing!" said Ellen. "Can you go through doors too?"

"Naturally, but someone seems to have left this one open."

"That's Luke. He's so irritating." Ellen closed the door and watched as Mirror-Belle glided through it and back again.

Splodge barked furiously.

"It's a pity you can't keep him under better control," said Mirror-Belle. "Still, I suppose I shouldn't expect your dog to be as well behaved as mine, seeing that he doesn't have any royal blood."

In fact, Mirror-Belle's dog, Prince Precious Paws, was the worst-behaved pet Ellen had ever met. She remembered the time he had stolen a roast chicken and scared a lot of sheep, but she decided not to mention this. Instead, now that they were on the subject of dogs, she found herself telling Mirror-Belle all about the Unusual Pets Club and how annoying Crystal was.

"And Luke's been horrible too," she said. "Everyone seems to be against me."

A thoughtful look crossed Mirror-Belle's

face. "I can change that," she said, and she walked through the television.

Splodge began to bark at the television as if this should have stopped Mirror-Belle.

"Calm down," Ellen told him, but Mirror-Belle said, "He needs to look at the television. It's part of the plan."

Just then, a strange echoey barking sound came from the screen.

"Here he comes, the dear sweet creature," Mirror-Belle said, and the next second a ghostly Prince Precious Paws bounded out of the screen and into the room.

"There's your unusual pet," said Mirror-Belle to Ellen. "At least, he's mine, really, but I'll let you borrow him."

Luke was hungry. Supper wouldn't be for ages: Mum was still teaching the piano. He opened the kitchen cupboard and  found a jar of salsa.

"But I can see a big wave coming

And it's gonna crash over you," he sang as he rummaged around some more. That Fire Engine song was so brilliant. Luke

 151

wished he could write something as good as that for his own band, Breakneck.

He discovered a bag of rather stale crisps and dipped one into the bright red salsa. Suddenly he felt inspired. "Red, the colour of anger," he said to himself. That would be a good first line. How could the song go after that?

"Red, the colour of anger,

Blue, the colour of sorrow . . ." he sang with his mouth full. He was pausing to think what could come next, when a soft, eerie voice behind him sang:

"And green for the mean, mean brother

Who wouldn't let his sister borrow."

Luke looked over his shoulder and saw Ellen. At least, he thought he saw her, but the next second she had gone. She seemed

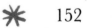

to have disappeared through the wall. But of course she couldn't have done that.

"Ellen!" Luke strode out of the kitchen and into the television room. Only Splodge was there, sitting in front of the television and staring at the blank screen. Ellen was probably hiding somewhere, giggling. Oh well, he wouldn't give her the satisfaction of looking for her. Better make a start on his homework.

Up in his room, Luke found it hard to concentrate on the Second World War. He kept thinking about Ellen and feeling a bit guilty that he hadn't let her borrow his pet.

Evilton was burrowing about in the bark chippings inside his tank on Luke's table. As Luke watched him the words of a

new song began to form themselves in his mind.

"You just want to poison me

But I'm not gonna let you start . . ."

He chewed his pen and wondered how to carry on. Then his skin prickled as he heard the same ghostly voice as before.

"You just want to poison me

And I'm dying of a broken heart."

Luke jumped up and turned round. There stood Ellen, and yet he hadn't heard her come into the room.

"Ellen – why can't you knock

before you . . ." Luke's voice trailed off and he stared at his sister. With a cold shock, he realized he could see right through her.

"Ellen, what's the matter . . . you look all . . . You look like a . . ." Luke couldn't bring himself to say the word "ghost".

The ghostly girl gave a small sad smile. "I forgive you," she said, "but can you forgive yourself?"

Luke gaped. The girl was stepping backwards, still fixing him with her haunting gaze. Then, before he could think what to say, she had

vanished through his bedroom wall.

He shivered. What was happening?

"Ellen! Come back!" But had it been Ellen?

Maybe Luke had just been thinking so deeply about his new song that he had somehow imagined his sister's ghost. But why? It was strange, even frightening.

Luke searched the house. He could hear piano music coming from the sitting room, and in the television room Splodge was still staring at the blank screen, but there was no sign of Ellen. The more Luke thought about her the more he wished he had been nicer to her.

Then he saw the note on the hall table. "Gone to the Unusual Pets Club," it said.

So that was all right then. Or was it?

"Right, everyone's here," said Crystal.

"Except for Ellen," said Katy.

"Well, we'll just have to start without her."

Crystal's front room looked like a vet's waiting room. Five children were sitting around with their pets either on their knees or in boxes or cages beside them. Crystal, in the biggest armchair, had to keep moving one hand in front of the other as her hamster Silver ran over them.

"Welcome to the Unusual Pets Club," she said. "We'll take turns to introduce our pets, and then at the end of the meeting we'll vote for the most unusual one. The winner will get this special certificate." She let Katy take Silver while she held out a piece of paper with "Most Unusual Pet of the Week" written on it in big purple letters.

"But won't the same pet just win every week?" asked Martin Booth, whose pet slow-worm was draped contentedly round his neck.

"Not necessarily. New people might join, or someone might get a new pet, or . . . well, some pets might just become more unusual. Now, we'll go round in a circle, starting with me." Crystal took Silver back from Katy and explained about his unusual feeding habits. She gave him two pieces of carrot, and sure enough he stuffed them both into his right pouch. Some people clapped, and Crystal smiled smugly.

"You next, Rachel."

Rachel had brought a Siamese cat who was sitting on her knee.

"This is Lapsang," she said. "She's got a very unusual miaow."

"What's unusual about it?" demanded Crystal.

"It's very low. She sounds more like a dog than a cat."

"But all Siamese cats have low voices," said Martin.

"Not as low as Lapsang's," said Rachel.

"Let's hear it then," Crystal ordered.

"Go on, Lapsang – miaow!" Rachel jiggled her legs, disturbing Lapsang's

 comfortable position. The cat looked offended, jumped off Rachel's lap and stalked silently to the door.

"She'll probably do it later," said Rachel, looking pleadingly at Crystal.

"She'll have to, otherwise you can't stay in the club," said Crystal. She turned to Martin. "Your turn."

"This is Sinclair," said Martin, unwinding his slow-worm from his neck and holding him out. Some of the other children backed away.

"Is he poisonous?" asked Rachel.

Martin gave her a scornful look. "No. He's not a snake. He's a slow-worm. That's

 160

a type of lizard – a legless lizard," he said triumphantly.

Everyone looked impressed apart from Crystal, who said, "Well, go on then. Tell us what's unusual about him."

"I've just told you. He hasn't got any legs. Most lizards have legs, don't they?"

"Yes, but slow-worms don't," pointed out Katy. "I think Sinclair would be more unusual if he did have legs."

An argument broke out, with the children taking sides. Crystal had to call the meeting to order.

"We can have the discussion and the vote at the end," she said. "Now, tell us about your guinea pig, Pamina."

"She's got very unusual fur," said Pamina, producing a mangy-looking

ginger guinea-pig from a box of straw.
"And she's also got a very unusual name –
Timbucktoodle-oo."

"Names don't count," Crystal told her.
"Tell us what's unusual about the fur."

"Well, you
can see," said
Pamina. "It's got
all these bald
patches."

"I don't call that
properly unusual," said Crystal. "I'd say
she's just got some kind of disease. You
ought to take her to the vet. Now, Katy,
it's your turn."

But before Katy's stick insect had a
chance to show off its dancing talent,
there was a ring at the door.

Crystal went to answer it. "Hello, Ellen. You're a bit late," the others heard her say, and the next second a strange-looking dog bounded into the room.

Lapsang's fur stood on end and she at last demonstrated her low-pitched miaow, but this didn't put the new unusual pet off: he made a dash for the cat, who fled across the room and up the curtains.

"Come here, Prince Precious . . . I mean, Splodge!" commanded Ellen, but the dog ignored her. He had spotted Silver the hamster and was leaping up at Crystal. Everyone gasped: for one second it looked as if his jaws had actually closed round the hamster. But a moment later the dog had bounded back to Ellen and Silver was still running about over Crystal's hands.

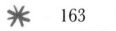

"Being unusually badly-behaved doesn't count," said Crystal.

"Is Splodge all right?" Katy asked Ellen. "He looks all different – sort of see-through."

"That's his new trick," said Ellen. "He can turn himself into a ghost dog."

Just then the dog gave a growl which was more like the rustle of autumn leaves. He was staring at Sinclair the slow-worm and his ghostly hair was bristling. He backed away, then turned and ran.

"He's gone through the wall!" exclaimed Rachel.

"He couldn't have done," said Crystal.

"He has," said Ellen. "He

can do that. He's a very, very unusual pet."

"There he is – he's looking in through the window!" said Martin.

Lapsang gave another deep miaow, then jumped down from the curtain and slunk into her cat basket.

"Call him back inside, Ellen," said Katy.

"I don't think he'll come if Sinclair is still out," said Ellen.

Martin obligingly put Sinclair into his tank and covered it with his jacket. Meanwhile Rachel put Timbucktoodle-oo back into his box and Crystal shut Silver into his cage. Then Ellen called, "Splodge! Splodge!" and the ghost dog came bounding in through the closed window.

Everyone laughed and clapped. After

that the children had fun getting Ellen's unusual pet to go through various bits of furniture.

"He can even go through people!" boasted Ellen. They all stood in a line, shoulder to shoulder, and sure enough the wildly excited dog jumped through the human wall and back again. After a few goes of this, he leaped through the window again.

"What's he up to now?" said Pamina.

They all crowded to the window. Crystal's little brother was outside, playing football with some friends. The ghost dog was trying to get the ball, but of course

his jaws just kept going through it.

"Come back!" Ellen called. The dog turned and gave her a cheeky look, and then he bounded off down the road. She guessed he was going back to his true owner but she didn't tell the others.

"As he's not here any more, no one's allowed to vote for him," said Crystal, but for once the others rose up against her: "That's not fair." "He was at the meeting." "He's so unusual!"

Crystal had to give in. "All right. But remember," and she glared at Ellen, "no one is allowed to vote for their own pet."

 167

The vote took place, and there was no doubt about the winner. Twiglet the stick insect got two votes (from Crystal and Ellen); everyone else voted for the ghost dog.

Rather grumpily, Crystal handed Ellen  the certificate. "I hope you realize that the winner has to have the next meeting in their house. It's in the rules," she said.

"That should be fine," said Ellen, "but I don't know if Splodge will be able to do his ghost trick next week. He only does it sometimes."

Everyone except Crystal looked disappointed.

Back home, Ellen had a quick look round
for the mirror girl and dog, but there was
no sign of them and Mum was calling her
to supper.

"Pass the potatoes, please, Ellen," said
Luke. "Did you have a good time at the
club?" He sounded surprisingly polite.

"Yes, thanks," said Ellen frostily. She
still hadn't forgiven him for his behaviour
earlier.

"What club?" asked
Dad, so Ellen told them
a bit about the meeting.
She didn't mention Prince
Precious Paws. Her family
didn't even believe in
Mirror-Belle, so she

reckoned that a ghost dog would be too much for them to swallow. Instead she pretended that she had just gone along to watch.

"Why didn't you take Splodge with you?" asked Mum.

"He's not unusual enough," Ellen explained. "But maybe I'll be able to teach him a couple of tricks by next week. The meeting's supposed to be here at six o'clock – is that all right?"

Mum agreed, and Luke said, "That's good. You'll have time to watch *Holiday Swap* first."

Ellen gave him a suspicious look. "Why are you being so nice all of a sudden?" she asked. "What's got into you?"

"Just toad-in-the-hole," said Luke,

holding out his plate for a second helping.

"Talking of television," said Dad, "Splodge was behaving very oddly when I was watching the news just now. He kept barking at the television, as if it was going to bite him. And then I noticed that the screen had paw prints on it, as if he'd been attacking it – all very weird."

Ellen smiled. She knew who the paw prints really belonged to. Prince Precious Paws must have gone back through the screen with Mirror-Belle. She felt sorry not to have said goodbye.

"Well, Ellen?" said Luke, breaking into her secret thoughts, and Ellen realized he had been talking to her.

"Sorry, I wasn't concentrating."

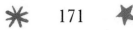

"I was just saying," said Luke, "that I've been thinking about Evilton. If you want to borrow him next week, that's fine by me."

About the Author

Julia Donaldson is one of the UK's most popular children's writers. Her award-winning books include *What the Ladybird Heard*, *The Detective Dog*, *The Snail and the Whale* and *The Gruffalo*. She has also written many children's plays and songs, and her sell-out shows based on her books and songs are a huge success. She was the Children's Laureate from 2011 to 2013, campaigning for libraries and for deaf children, and creating a website for teachers called picturebookplays.co.uk. Julia and her husband Malcolm divide their time between Sussex and Edinburgh. You can find out more about Julia at www.juliadonaldson.co.uk.

About the Illustrator

Lydia Monks studied Illustration at Kingston University, graduating in 1994 with a first-class degree. She is a former winner of the Smarties Bronze Award for *I Wish I Were a Dog* and has illustrated many books by Julia Donaldson. Her illustrations have been widely admired. You can find out more about Lydia at www.lydiamonks.com.

Have you read

Have you read

Have you read

For younger readers

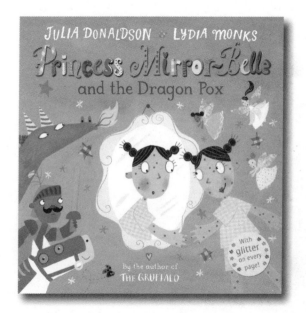